'WHAT MEN LIVE BY' AND OTHER TALES

LEO TOLSTOY

ISBN: 978-1496174932

Table of Contents

"We know that we have passed out of death into life, because we love the brethren. He that loveth not abideth in death." —1 "Epistle St. John" iii. 14.

"Whoso hath the world's goods, and beholdeth his brother in
need, and shutteth up his compassion from him, how doth the
love of God abide in him? My little children, let us not
love in word, neither with the tongue; but in deed and
truth." —iii. 17-18.

"Love is of God; and every one that loveth is begotten of
God, and knoweth God. He that loveth not knoweth not God;
for God is love." —iv. 7-8.

"No man hath beheld God at any time; if we love one another,
God abideth in us." —iv. 12.

"God is love; and he that abideth in love abideth in God,
and God abideth in him." —iv. 16.

"If a man say, I love God, and hateth his brother, he is a
liar; for he that loveth not his brother whom he hath seen,
how can he love God whom he hath not seen?" —iv. 20.

WHAT MEN LIVE BY

A shoemaker named Simon, who had neither house nor land of his own, lived with his wife and children in a peasant's hut, and earned his living by his work. Work was cheap, but bread was dear, and what he earned he spent for food. The man and his wife had but one sheepskin coat between them for winter wear, and even that was torn to tatters, and this was the second year he had been wanting to buy sheep-skins for a new coat. Before winter Simon saved up a little money: a three-rouble note lay hidden in his wife's box, and five roubles and twenty kopeks were owed him by customers in the village.

So one morning he prepared to go to the village to buy the sheep-skins. He put on over his shirt his wife's wadded nankeen jacket, and over that he put his own cloth coat. He took the three-rouble note in his pocket, cut himself a stick to serve as a staff, and started off after breakfast. "I'll collect the five roubles that are due to me," thought he, "add the three I have got, and that will be enough to buy sheep-skins for the winter coat."

He came to the village and called at a peasant's hut, but the man was not at home. The peasant's wife promised that the money should be paid next week, but she would not pay it herself. Then Simon called on another peasant, but this one swore he had no money, and would only pay twenty kopeks which he owed for a pair of boots Simon had mended. Simon then tried to buy the sheep-skins on credit, but the dealer would not trust him.

"Bring your money," said he, "then you may have your pick of the skins. We know what debt-collecting is like." So all the business the shoemaker did was to get the twenty kopeks for boots he had mended, and to take a pair of felt boots a peasant gave him to sole with leather.

Simon felt downhearted. He spent the twenty kopeks on vodka, and started homewards without having bought any skins. In the morning he had felt the frost; but now, after drinking the vodka, he felt warm, even without a sheep-skin coat. He trudged along, striking his stick on the frozen earth with one hand, swinging the felt boots with the other, and talking to himself.

I

"I'm quite warm," said he, "though I have no sheep-skin coat. I've had a drop, and it runs through all my veins. I need no sheep-skins. I go along and don't worry about anything. That's the sort of man I am! What do I care? I can live without sheep-skins. I don't need them. My wife will fret, to be sure. And, true enough, it is a shame; one works all day long, and then does not get paid. Stop a bit! If you don't bring that money along, sure enough I'll skin you, blessed if I don't. How's that? He pays twenty kopeks at a time! What can I do with twenty kopeks? Drink it-that's all one can do! Hard up, he says he is! So he may be—but what about me? You have a house, and cattle, and everything; I've only what I stand up in! You have corn of your own growing; I have to buy every grain. Do what I will, I must spend three roubles every week for bread alone. I come home and find the bread all used up, and I have to fork out another rouble and a half. So just pay up what you owe, and no nonsense about it!"

By this time he had nearly reached the shrine at the bend of the road. Looking up, he saw something whitish behind the shrine. The daylight was fading, and the shoemaker peered at the thing without being able to make out what it was. "There was no white stone here before. Can it be an ox? It's not like an ox. It has a head like a man, but it's too white; and what could a man be doing there?"

He came closer, so that it was clearly visible. To his surprise it really was a man, alive or dead, sitting naked, leaning motionless against the shrine. Terror seized the shoemaker, and he thought, "Someone has killed him, stripped him, and left him there. If I meddle I shall surely get into trouble."

So the shoemaker went on. He passed in front of the shrine so that he could not see the man. When he had gone some way, he looked back, and saw that the man was no longer leaning against the shrine, but was moving as if looking towards him. The shoemaker felt more frightened than before, and thought, "Shall I go back to him, or shall I go on? If I go near him something dreadful may happen. Who knows who the fellow is? He has not come here for any good. If I go near him he may jump up and throttle me, and there will be no getting away. Or if not, he'd still be a burden on one's hands. What could I do with a naked man? I couldn't give him my last clothes. Heaven only help me to get away!"

So the shoemaker hurried on, leaving the shrine behind him-when suddenly his conscience smote him, and he stopped in the road.

"What are you doing, Simon?" said he to himself. "The man may be dying of want, and you slip past afraid. Have you grown so rich as to be afraid of robbers? Ah, Simon, shame on you!"

So he turned back and went up to the man.

II

Simon approached the stranger, looked at him, and saw that he was a young man, fit, with no bruises on his body, only evidently freezing and frightened, and he sat there leaning back without looking up at Simon, as if too faint to lift his eyes. Simon went close to him, and then the man seemed to wake up. Turning his head, he opened his eyes and looked into Simon's face. That one look was enough to make Simon fond of the man. He threw the felt boots on the ground, undid his sash, laid it on the boots, and took off his cloth coat.

"It's not a time for talking," said he. "Come, put this coat on at once!" And Simon took the man by the elbows and helped him to rise. As he stood there, Simon saw that his body was clean and in good condition, his hands and feet shapely, and his face good and kind. He threw his coat over the man's shoulders, but the latter could not find the sleeves. Simon guided his arms into them, and drawing the coat well on, wrapped it closely about him, tying the sash round the man's waist.

Simon even took off his torn cap to put it on the man's head, but then his own head felt cold, and he thought: "I'm quite bald, while he has long curly hair." So he put his cap on his own head again. "It will be better to give him something for his feet," thought he; and he made the man sit down, and helped him to put on the felt boots, saying, "There, friend, now move about and warm yourself. Other matters can be settled later on. Can you walk?"

The man stood up and looked kindly at Simon, but could not say a word.

"Why don't you speak?" said Simon. "It's too cold to stay here, we must be getting home. There now, take my stick, and if you're feeling weak, lean on that. Now step out!"

The man started walking, and moved easily, not lagging behind.

As they went along, Simon asked him, "And where do you belong to?" "I'm not from these parts."

"I thought as much. I know the folks hereabouts. But, how did you come to be there by the shrine?"

"I cannot tell."

"Has some one been ill-treating you?"

"No one has ill-treated me. God has punished me."

"Of course God rules all. Still, you'll have to find food and shelter somewhere. Where do you want to go to?"

"It is all the same to me."

Simon was amazed. The man did not look like a rogue, and he spoke gently, but yet he gave no account of himself. Still Simon thought, "Who knows what may have happened?" And he said to the stranger: "Well then, come home with me, and at least warm yourself awhile."

So Simon walked towards his home, and the stranger kept up with him, walking at his side. The wind had risen and Simon felt it cold under his shirt. He was getting over his tipsiness by now, and began to feel the frost. He went along sniffling and wrapping his wife's coat round him, and he thought to himself: "There now—talk about sheep-skins! I went out for sheep-skins and come home without even a coat to my back, and what is more, I'm bringing a naked man along with me. Matryona won't be pleased!" And when he thought of his wife he felt sad; but when he looked at the stranger and remembered how he had looked up at him at the shrine, his heart was glad.

III

Simon's wife had everything ready early that day. She had cut wood, brought water, fed the children, eaten her own meal, and now she sat thinking. She wondered when she ought to make bread: now or tomorrow? There was still a large piece left.

"If Simon has had some dinner in town," thought she, "and does not eat much for supper, the bread will last out another day."

She weighed the piece of bread in her hand again and again, and thought: "I won't make any more today. We have only enough flour left to bake one batch; We can manage to make this last out till Friday."

So Matryona put away the bread, and sat down at the table to patch her husband's shirt. While she worked she thought how her husband was buying skins for a winter coat.

"If only the dealer does not cheat him. My good man is much too simple; he cheats nobody, but any child can take him in. Eight roubles is a lot of money—he should get a good coat at that price. Not tanned skins, but still a proper winter coat. How difficult it was last winter to get on without a warm coat. I could neither get down to the river, nor go out anywhere. When he went out he put on all we had, and there was nothing left for me. He did not start very early today, but still it's time he was back. I only hope he has not gone on the spree!"

Hardly had Matryona thought this, when steps were heard on the threshold, and some one entered. Matryona stuck her needle into her work and went out into the passage. There she saw two men: Simon, and with him a man without a hat, and wearing felt boots.

Matryona noticed at once that her husband smelt of spirits. "There now, he has been drinking," thought she. And when she saw that he was coatless, had only her jacket on, brought no parcel, stood there silent, and seemed ashamed, her heart was ready to break with disappointment. "He has drunk the money," thought she, "and has been on the spree with some good-for-nothing fellow whom he has brought home with him."

Matryona let them pass into the hut, followed them in, and saw that the stranger was a young, slight man, wearing her husband's coat. There was no shirt to be seen under it, and he had no hat. Having entered, he stood, neither moving, nor raising his eyes, and Matryona thought: "He must be a bad man—he's afraid."

Matryona frowned, and stood beside the oven looking to see what they would do.

Simon took off his cap and sat down on the bench as if things were all right.

"Come, Matryona; if supper is ready, let us have some."

Matryona muttered something to herself and did not move, but stayed where she was, by the oven. She looked first at the one and then at the other of them, and only shook her head. Simon saw that his wife was annoyed, but tried to pass it off. Pretending not to notice anything, he took the stranger by the arm.

"Sit down, friend," said he, "and let us have some supper."

The stranger sat down on the bench.

"Haven't you cooked anything for us?" said Simon.

Matryona's anger boiled over. "I've cooked, but not for you. It seems to me you have drunk your wits away. You went to buy a sheep-skin coat, but come home without so much as the coat you had on, and bring a naked vagabond home with you. I have no supper for drunkards like you."

"That's enough, Matryona. Don't wag your tongue without reason. You had better ask what sort of man—"

"And you tell me what you've done with the money?"

Simon found the pocket of the jacket, drew out the three-rouble note, and unfolded it.

"Here is the money. Trifonof did not pay, but promises to pay soon."

Matryona got still more angry; he had bought no sheep-skins, but had put his only coat on some naked fellow and had even brought him to their house.

She snatched up the note from the table, took it to put away in safety, and said: "I have no supper for you. We can't feed all the naked drunkards in the world."

"There now, Matryona, hold your tongue a bit. First hear what a man has to say-"

"Much wisdom I shall hear from a drunken fool. I was right in not wanting to marry you-a drunkard. The linen my mother gave me you drank; and now you've been to buy a coat-and have drunk it, too!"

Simon tried to explain to his wife that he had only spent twenty kopeks; tried to tell how he had found the man—but Matryona would not let him get a word in. She talked nineteen to the dozen, and dragged in things that had happened ten years before.

Matryona talked and talked, and at last she flew at Simon and seized him by the sleeve.

"Give me my jacket. It is the only one I have, and you must needs take it from me and wear it yourself. Give it here, you mangy dog, and may the devil take you."

Simon began to pull off the jacket, and turned a sleeve of it inside out; Matryona seized the jacket and it burst its seams, She snatched it up, threw it over her head and went to the door. She meant to go out, but stopped undecided—she wanted to work off her anger, but she also wanted to learn what sort of a man the stranger was.

IV

Matryona stopped and said: "If he were a good man he would not be naked. Why, he hasn't even a shirt on him. If he were all right, you would say where you came across the fellow."

"That's just what I am trying to tell you," said Simon. "As I came to the shrine I saw him sitting all naked and frozen. It isn't quite the weather to sit about naked! God sent me to him, or he would have perished. What was I to do? How do we know what may have happened to him? So I took him, clothed him, and brought him along. Don't be so angry, Matryona. It is a sin. Remember, we all must die one day."

Angry words rose to Matryona's lips, but she looked at the stranger and was silent. He sat on the edge of the bench, motionless, his hands folded on his knees, his head drooping on his breast, his eyes closed, and his brows knit as if in pain. Matryona was silent: and Simon said: "Matryona, have you no love of God?"

Matryona heard these words, and as she looked at the stranger, suddenly her heart softened towards him. She came back from the door, and going to the oven she got out the supper. Setting a cup on the table, she poured out some kvas. Then she brought out the last piece of bread, and set out a knife and spoons.

"Eat, if you want to," said she.

Simon drew the stranger to the table.

"Take your place, young man," said he.

Simon cut the bread, crumbled it into the broth, and they began to eat. Matryona sat at the corner of the table resting her head on her hand and looking at the stranger.

And Matryona was touched with pity for the stranger, and began to feel fond of him. And at once the stranger's face lit up; his brows were no longer bent, he raised his eyes and smiled at Matryona.

When they had finished supper, the woman cleared away the things and began questioning the stranger. "Where are you from?" said she.

"I am not from these parts."

"But how did you come to be on the road?"

"I may not tell."

"Did some one rob you?"

"God punished me."

"And you were lying there naked?"

"Yes, naked and freezing. Simon saw me and had pity on me. He took off his coat, put it on me and brought me here. And you have fed me, given me drink, and shown pity on me. God will reward you!"

Matryona rose, took from the window Simon's old shirt she had been patching, and gave it to the stranger. She also brought out a pair of trousers for him.

"There," said she, "I see you have no shirt. Put this on, and lie down where you please, in the loft or on the oven."

The stranger took off the coat, put on the shirt, and lay down in the loft. Matryona put out the candle, took the coat, and climbed to where her husband lay.

Matryona drew the skirts of the coat over her and lay down, but could not sleep; she could not get the stranger out of her mind.

When she remembered that he had eaten their last piece of bread and that there was none for tomorrow, and thought of the shirt and trousers she had given away, she felt grieved; but when she remembered how he had smiled, her heart was glad.

Long did Matryona lie awake, and she noticed that Simon also was awake—he drew the coat towards him.

"Simon!"

"Well?"

"You have had the last of the bread, and I have not put any to rise. I don't know what we shall do tomorrow. Perhaps I can borrow some of neighbor Martha."

"If we're alive we shall find something to eat."

The woman lay still awhile, and then said, "He seems a good man, but why does he not tell us who he is?"

"I suppose he has his reasons."

"Simon!"

"Well?"

"We give; but why does nobody give us anything?"

Simon did not know what to say; so he only said, "Let us stop talking," and turned over and went to sleep.

V

In the morning Simon awoke. The children were still asleep; his wife had gone to the neighbor's to borrow some bread. The stranger alone was sitting on the bench, dressed in the old shirt and trousers, and looking upwards. His face was brighter than it had been the day before.

Simon said to him, "Well, friend; the belly wants bread, and the naked body clothes. One has to work for a living What work do you know?"

"I do not know any."

This surprised Simon, but he said, "Men who want to learn can learn anything."

"Men work, and I will work also."

"What is your name?"

"Michael."

"Well, Michael, if you don't wish to talk about yourself, that is your own affair; but you'll have to earn a living for yourself. If you will work as I tell you, I will give you food and shelter."

"May God reward you! I will learn. Show me what to do."

Simon took yarn, put it round his thumb and began to twist it.

"It is easy enough—see!"

Michael watched him, put some yarn round his own thumb in the same way, caught the knack, and twisted the yarn also.

Then Simon showed him how to wax the thread. This also Michael mastered. Next Simon showed him how to twist the bristle in, and how to sew, and this, too, Michael learned at once.

Whatever Simon showed him he understood at once, and after three days he worked as if he had sewn boots all his life. He worked without stopping, and ate little. When work was over he sat silently, looking upwards. He hardly went into the street, spoke only when necessary, and neither joked nor laughed. They never saw him smile, except that first evening when Matryona gave them supper.

VI

Day by day and week by week the year went round. Michael lived and worked with Simon. His fame spread till people said that no one sewed boots so neatly and strongly as Simon's workman, Michael; and from all the district round people came to Simon for their boots, and he began to be well off.

One winter day, as Simon and Michael sat working, a carriage on sledge-runners, with three horses and with bells, drove up to the hut. They looked out of the window; the carriage stopped at their door, a fine servant jumped down from the box and opened the door. A gentleman in a fur coat got out and walked up to Simon's hut. Up jumped Matryona and opened the door wide. The gentleman stooped to enter the hut, and when he drew himself up again his head nearly reached the ceiling, and he seemed quite to fill his end of the room.

Simon rose, bowed, and looked at the gentleman with astonishment. He had never seen any one like him. Simon himself was lean, Michael was thin, and Matryona was dry as a bone, but this man was like some one from another world: red-faced, burly, with a neck like a bull's, and looking altogether as if he were cast in iron.

The gentleman puffed, threw off his fur coat, sat down on the bench, and said, "Which of you is the master bootmaker?"

"I am, your Excellency," said Simon, coming forward.

Then the gentleman shouted to his lad, "Hey, Fedka, bring the leather!"

The servant ran in, bringing a parcel. The gentleman took the parcel and put it on the table.

"Untie it," said he. The lad untied it.

The gentleman pointed to the leather.

"Look here, shoemaker," said he, "do you see this leather?"

"Yes, your honor."

"But do you know what sort of leather it is?"

Simon felt the leather and said, "It is good leather."

"Good, indeed! Why, you fool, you never saw such leather before in your life. It's German, and cost twenty roubles."

Simon was frightened, and said, "Where should I ever see leather like that?"

"Just so! Now, can you make it into boots for me?"

"Yes, your Excellency, I can."

Then the gentleman shouted at him: "You can, can you? Well, remember whom you are to make them for, and what the leather is. You must make me boots that will wear for a year, neither losing shape nor coming unsown. If you can do it, take the leather and cut it up; but if you can't, say so. I warn you now if your boots become unsewn or lose shape within a year, I will have you put in prison. If they don't burst or lose shape for a year I will pay you ten roubles for your work."

Simon was frightened, and did not know what to say. He glanced at Michael and nudging him with his elbow, whispered: "Shall I take the work?"

Michael nodded his head as if to say, "Yes, take it."

Simon did as Michael advised, and undertook to make boots that would not lose shape or split for a whole year.

Calling his servant, the gentleman told him to pull the boot off his left leg, which he stretched out.

"Take my measure!" said he.

Simon stitched a paper measure seventeen inches long, smoothed it out, knelt down, wiped his hand well on his apron so as not to soil the gentleman's sock, and began to measure. He measured the sole, and round the instep, and began to measure the calf of the leg, but the paper was too short. The calf of the leg was as thick as a beam.

"Mind you don't make it too tight in the leg."

Simon stitched on another strip of paper. The gentleman twitched his toes about in his sock, looking round at those in the hut, and as he did so he noticed Michael.

"Whom have you there?" asked he.

"That is my workman. He will sew the boots."

"Mind," said the gentleman to Michael, "remember to make them so that they will last me a year."

Simon also looked at Michael, and saw that Michael was not looking at the gentleman, but was gazing into the corner behind the gentleman, as if he saw some one there. Michael looked and looked, and suddenly he smiled, and his face became brighter.

"What are you grinning at, you fool?" thundered the gentleman. "You had better look to it that the boots are ready in time."

"They shall be ready in good time," said Michael.

"Mind it is so," said the gentleman, and he put on his boots and his fur coat, wrapped the latter round him, and went to the door. But he forgot to stoop, and struck his head against the lintel.

He swore and rubbed his head. Then he took his seat in the carriage and drove away.

When he had gone, Simon said: "There's a figure of a man for you! You could not kill him with a mallet. He almost knocked out the lintel, but little harm it did him."

And Matryona said: "Living as he does, how should he not grow strong? Death itself can't touch such a rock as that."

VII

Then Simon said to Michael: "Well, we have taken the work, but we must see we don't get into trouble over it. The leather is dear, and the gentleman hot-tempered. We must make no mistakes. Come, your eye is truer and your hands have become nimbler than mine, so you take this measure and cut out the boots. I will finish off the sewing of the vamps."

Michael did as he was told. He took the leather, spread it out on the table, folded it in two, took a knife and began to cut out.

Matryona came and watched him cutting, and was surprised to see how he was doing it. Matryona was accustomed to seeing boots made, and she looked and saw that Michael was not cutting the leather for boots, but was cutting it round.

She wished to say something, but she thought to herself: "Perhaps I do not understand how gentleman's boots should be made. I suppose Michael knows more about it—and I won't interfere."

When Michael had cut up the leather, he took a thread and began to sew not with two ends, as boots are sewn, but with a single end, as for soft slippers.

Again Matryona wondered, but again she did not interfere. Michael sewed on steadily till noon. Then Simon rose for dinner, looked around, and saw that Michael had made slippers out of the gentleman's leather.

"Ah," groaned Simon, and he thought, "How is it that Michael, who has been with me a whole year and never made a mistake before, should do such a dreadful thing? The gentleman ordered high boots, welted, with whole fronts, and Michael has made soft slippers with single soles, and has wasted the leather. What am I to say to the gentleman? I can never replace leather such as this."

And he said to Michael, "What are you doing, friend? You have ruined me! You know the gentleman ordered high boots, but see what you have made!"

Hardly had he begun to rebuke Michael, when "rat-tat" went the iron ring that hung at the door. Some one was knocking. They looked out of the window; a man had come on horseback, and was fastening his horse. They opened the door, and the servant who had been with the gentleman came in.

"Good day," said he.

"Good day," replied Simon. "What can we do for you?"

"My mistress has sent me about the boots."

"What about the boots?"

"Why, my master no longer needs them. He is dead."

"Is it possible?"

"He did not live to get home after leaving you, but died in the carriage. When we reached home and the servants came to help him alight, he rolled over like a sack. He was dead already, and so stiff that he could hardly be got out of the carriage. My mistress sent me here, saying: 'Tell the bootmaker that the gentleman who ordered boots of him and left the leather for them no longer needs the boots, but that he must quickly make soft slippers for the corpse. Wait till they are ready, and bring them back with you.' That is why I have come."

Michael gathered up the remnants of the leather; rolled them up, took the soft slippers he had made, slapped them together, wiped them down with his apron, and handed them and the roll of leather to the servant, who took them and said: "Good-bye, masters, and good day to you!"

VIII

Another year passed, and another, and Michael was now living his sixth year with Simon. He lived as before. He went nowhere, only spoke when necessary, and had only smiled twice in all those years—once when Matryona gave him food, and a second time when the gentleman was in their hut. Simon was more than pleased with his workman. He never now asked him where he came from, and only feared lest Michael should go away.

They were all at home one day. Matryona was putting iron pots in the oven; the children were running along the benches and looking out of the window; Simon was sewing at one window, and Michael was fastening on a heel at the other.

One of the boys ran along the bench to Michael, leant on his shoulder, and looked out of the window.

"Look, Uncle Michael! There is a lady with little girls! She seems to be coming here. And one of the girls is lame."

When the boy said that, Michael dropped his work, turned to the window, and looked out into the street.

Simon was surprised. Michael never used to look out into the street, but now he pressed against the window, staring at something. Simon also looked out, and saw that a well-dressed woman was really coming to his hut, leading by the hand two little girls in fur coats and woolen shawls. The girls could hardly be told one from the other, except that one of them was crippled in her left leg and walked with a limp.

The woman stepped into the porch and entered the passage. Feeling about for the entrance she found the latch, which she lifted, and opened the door. She let the two girls go in first, and followed them into the hut.

"Good day, good folk!"

"Pray come in," said Simon. "What can we do for you?"

The woman sat down by the table. The two little girls pressed close to her knees, afraid of the people in the hut.

"I want leather shoes made for these two little girls for spring."

"We can do that. We never have made such small shoes, but we can make them; either welted or turnover shoes, linen lined. My man, Michael, is a master at the work."

Simon glanced at Michael and saw that he had left his work and was sitting with his eyes fixed on the little girls. Simon was surprised. It was true the girls were pretty, with black eyes, plump, and rosy-cheeked, and they wore nice kerchiefs and fur coats, but still Simon could not understand why Michael should look at them like that—just as if he had known them before. He was puzzled, but went on talking with the woman, and arranging the price. Having fixed it, he prepared the measure. The woman lifted the lame girl on to her lap and said: "Take two measures from this little girl. Make one shoe for the lame foot and three for the sound one. They both have the same size feet. They are twins."

Simon took the measure and, speaking of the lame girl, said: "How did it happen to her? She is such a pretty girl. Was she born so?"

"No, her mother crushed her leg."

Then Matryona joined in. She wondered who this woman was, and whose the children were, so she said: "Are not you their mother then?"

"No, my good woman; I am neither their mother nor any relation to them. They were quite strangers to me, but I adopted them."

"They are not your children and yet you are so fond of them?"

"How can I help being fond of them? I fed them both at my own breasts. I had a child of my own, but God took him. I was not so fond of him as I now am of them."

"Then whose children are they?"

IX
The woman, having begun talking, told them the whole story.

"It is about six years since their parents died, both in one week: their father was buried on the Tuesday, and their mother died on the Friday.

These orphans were born three days after their father's death, and their mother did not live another day. My husband and I were then living as peasants in the village. We were neighbors of theirs, our yard being next to theirs. Their father was a lonely man; a wood-cutter in the forest. When felling trees one day, they let one fall on him. It fell across his body and crushed his bowels out. They hardly got him home before his soul went to God; and that same week his wife gave birth to twins— these little girls. She was poor and alone; she had no one, young or old, with her. Alone she gave them birth, and alone she met her death."

"The next morning I went to see her, but when I entered the hut, she, poor thing, was already stark and cold. In dying she had rolled on to this child and crushed her leg. The village folk came to the hut, washed the body, laid her out, made a coffin, and buried her. They were good folk. The babies were left alone. What was to be done with them? I was the only woman there who had a baby at the time. I was nursing my first-born—eight weeks old. So I took them for a time. The peasants came together, and thought and thought what to do with them; and at last they said to me: 'For the present, Mary, you had better keep the girls, and later on we will arrange what to do for them.' So I nursed the sound one at my breast, but at first I did not feed this crippled one. I did not suppose she would live. But then I thought to myself, why should the poor innocent suffer? I pitied her, and began to feed her. And so I fed my own boy and these two—the three of them—at my own breast. I was young and strong, and had good food, and God gave me so much milk that at times it even overflowed. I used sometimes to feed two at a time, while the third was waiting. When one had enough I nursed the third. And God so ordered it that these grew up, while my own was buried before he was two years old. And I had no more children, though we prospered. Now my husband is working for the corn merchant at the mill. The pay is good, and we are well off. But I have no children of my own, and how lonely I should be without these little girls! How can I help loving them! They are the joy of my life!"

She pressed the lame little girl to her with one hand, while with the other she wiped the tears from her cheeks.

And Matryona sighed, and said: "The proverb is true that says, 'One may live without father or mother, but one cannot live without God.'"

So they talked together, when suddenly the whole hut was lighted up as though by summer lightning from the corner where Michael sat. They all looked towards him and saw him sitting, his hands folded on his knees, gazing upwards and smiling.

X

The woman went away with the girls. Michael rose from the bench, put down his work, and took off his apron. Then, bowing low to Simon and his wife, he said: "Farewell, masters. God has forgiven me. I ask your forgiveness, too, for anything done amiss."

And they saw that a light shone from Michael. And Simon rose, bowed down to Michael, and said: "I see, Michael, that you are no common man, and I can neither keep you nor question you. Only tell me this: how is it that when I found you and brought you home, you were gloomy, and when my wife gave you food you smiled at her and became brighter? Then when the gentleman came to order the boots, you smiled again and became brighter still? And now, when this woman brought the little girls, you smiled a third time, and have become as bright as day? Tell me, Michael, why does your face shine so, and why did you smile those three times?"

And Michael answered: "Light shines from me because I have been punished, but now God has pardoned me. And I smiled three times, because God sent me to learn three truths, and I have learnt them. One I learnt when your wife pitied me, and that is why I smiled the first time. The second I learnt when the rich man ordered the boots, and then I smiled again. And now, when I saw those little girls, I learn the third and last truth, and I smiled the third time."

And Simon said, "Tell me, Michael, what did God punish you for? and what were the three truths? that I, too, may know them."

And Michael answered: "God punished me for disobeying Him. I was an angel in heaven and disobeyed God. God sent me to fetch a woman's soul. I flew to earth, and saw a sick woman lying alone, who had just given birth to twin girls. They moved feebly at their mother's side, but she could not lift them to her breast. When she saw me, she understood that God had sent me for her soul, and she wept and said: 'Angel of God! My husband has just been buried, killed by a falling tree. I have neither sister, nor aunt, nor mother: no one to care for my orphans. Do not take my soul! Let me nurse my babes, feed them, and set them on their feet before I die. Children cannot live without father or mother.' And I hearkened to her. I placed one child at her breast and gave the other into her arms, and returned to the Lord in heaven. I flew to the Lord, and said: 'I could not take the soul of the mother. Her husband was killed by a tree; the woman has twins, and prays that her soul may not be taken. She says: "Let me nurse and feed my children, and set them on their feet. Children cannot live without father or mother." I have not taken her soul.' And God said: 'Go-take the mother's soul, and learn three truths: Learn What dwells in man, What is not given to man, and What men live by. When thou has learnt these things, thou shalt return to heaven.' So I flew again to earth and took the mother's soul. The babes dropped from her breasts. Her body rolled over on the bed and crushed one babe, twisting its leg. I rose above the village, wishing to take her soul to God; but a wind seized me, and my wings drooped and dropped off. Her soul rose alone to God, while I fell to earth by the roadside."

XI

And Simon and Matryona understood who it was that had lived with them, and whom they had clothed and fed. And they wept with awe and with joy. And the angel said: "I was alone in the field, naked. I had never known human needs, cold and hunger, till I became a man. I was famished, frozen, and did not know what to do. I saw, near the field I was in, a shrine built for God, and I went to it hoping to find shelter. But the shrine was locked, and I could not enter. So I sat down behind the shrine to shelter myself at least from the wind. Evening drew on. I was hungry, frozen, and in pain. Suddenly I heard a man coming along the road. He carried a pair of boots, and was talking to himself. For the first time since I became a man I saw the mortal face of a man, and his face seemed terrible to me and I turned from it. And I heard the man talking to himself of how to cover his body from the cold in winter, and how to feed wife and children. And I thought: 'I am perishing of cold and hunger, and here is a man thinking only of how to clothe himself and his wife, and how to get bread for themselves. He cannot help me.' When the man saw me he frowned and became still more terrible, and passed me by on the other side. I despaired; but suddenly I heard him coming back. I looked up, and did not recognize the same man; before, I had seen death in his face; but now he was alive, and I recognized in him the presence of God. He came up to me, clothed me, took me with him, and brought me to his home. I entered the house; a woman came to meet us and began to speak. The woman was still more terrible than the man had been; the spirit of death came from her mouth; I could not breathe for the stench of death that spread around her. She wished to drive me out into the cold, and I knew that if she did so she would die. Suddenly her husband spoke to her of God, and the woman changed at once. And when she brought me food and looked at me, I glanced at her and saw that death no longer dwelt in her; she had become alive, and in her, too, I saw God.

"Then I remembered the first lesson God had set me: 'Learn what dwells in man.' And I understood that in man dwells Love! I was glad that God had already begun to show me what He had promised, and I smiled for the first time. But I had not yet learnt all. I did not yet know What is not given to man, and What men live by.

"I lived with you, and a year passed. A man came to order boots that should wear for a year without losing shape or cracking. I looked at him, and suddenly, behind his shoulder, I saw my comrade—the angel of death. None but me saw that angel; but I knew him, and knew that before the sun set he would take that rich man's soul. And I thought to myself, 'The man is making preparations for a year, and does not know that he will die before evening.' And I remembered God's second saying, 'Learn what is not given to man.'

"What dwells in man I already knew. Now I learnt what is not given him. It is not given to man to know his own needs. And I smiled for the second time. I was glad to have seen my comrade angel—glad also that God had revealed to me the second saying.

"But I still did not know all. I did not know What men live by. And I lived on, waiting till God should reveal to me the last lesson. In the sixth year came the girl-twins with the woman; and I recognized the girls, and heard how they had been kept alive. Having heard the story, I thought, 'Their mother besought me for the children's sake, and I believed her when she said that children cannot live without father or mother; but a stranger has nursed them, and has brought them up.' And when the woman showed her love for the children that were not her own, and wept over them, I saw in her the living God and understood What men live by. And I knew that God had revealed to me the last lesson, and had forgiven my sin. And then I smiled for the third time."

XII

And the angel's body was bared, and he was clothed in light so that eye could not look on him; and his voice grew louder, as though it came not from him but from heaven above. And the angel said:

"I have learnt that all men live not by care for themselves but by love.

"It was not given to the mother to know what her children needed for their life. Nor was it given to the rich man to know what he himself needed. Nor is it given to any man to know whether, when evening comes, he will need boots for his body or slippers for his corpse.

"I remained alive when I was a man, not by care of myself, but because love was present in a passer-by, and because he and his wife pitied and loved me. The orphans remained alive not because of their mother's care, but because there was love in the heart of a woman, a stranger to them, who pitied and loved them. And all men live not by the thought they spend on their own welfare, but because love exists in man.

"I knew before that God gave life to men and desires that they should live; now I understood more than that.

"I understood that God does not wish men to live apart, and therefore he does not reveal to them what each one needs for himself; but he wishes them to live united, and therefore reveals to each of them what is necessary for all.

"I have now understood that though it seems to men that they live by care for themselves, in truth it is love alone by which they live. He who has love, is in God, and God is in him, for God is love."

And the angel sang praise to God, so that the hut trembled at his voice. The roof opened, and a column of fire rose from earth to heaven. Simon and his wife and children fell to the ground. Wings appeared upon the angel's shoulders, and he rose into the heavens.

And when Simon came to himself the hut stood as before, and there was no one in it but his own family.

THREE QUESTIONS

It once occurred to a certain king, that if he always knew the right time to begin everything; if he knew who were the right people to listen to, and whom to avoid; and, above all, if he always knew what was the most important thing to do, he would never fail in anything he might undertake.

And this thought having occurred to him, he had it proclaimed throughout his kingdom that he would give a great reward to any one who would teach him what was the right time for every action, and who were the most necessary people, and how he might know what was the most important thing to do.

And learned men came to the King, but they all answered his questions differently.

In reply to the first question, some said that to know the right time for every action, one must draw up in advance, a table of days, months and years, and must live strictly according to it. Only thus, said they, could everything be done at its proper time. Others declared that it was impossible to decide beforehand the right time for every action; but that, not letting oneself be absorbed in idle pastimes, one should always attend to all that was going on, and then do what was most needful. Others, again, said that however attentive the King might be to what was going on, it was impossible for one man to decide correctly the right time for every action, but that he should have a Council of wise men, who would help him to fix the proper time for everything.

But then again others said there were some things which could not wait to be laid before a Council, but about which one had at once to decide whether to undertake them or not. But in order to decide that, one must know beforehand what was going to happen. It is only magicians who know that; and, therefore, in order to know the right time for every action, one must consult magicians.

Equally various were the answers to the second question. Some said, the people the King most needed were his councillors; others, the priests; others, the doctors; while some said the warriors were the most necessary.

To the third question, as to what was the most important occupation: some replied that the most important thing in the world was science. Others said it was skill in warfare; and others, again, that it was religious worship.

All the answers being different, the King agreed with none of them, and gave the reward to none. But still wishing to find the right answers to his questions, he decided to consult a hermit, widely renowned for his wisdom.

The hermit lived in a wood which he never quitted, and he received none but common folk. So the King put on simple clothes, and before reaching the hermit's cell dismounted from his horse, and, leaving his body-guard behind, went on alone.

When the King approached, the hermit was digging the ground in front of his hut. Seeing the King, he greeted him and went on digging. The hermit was frail and weak, and each time he stuck his spade into the ground and turned a little earth, he breathed heavily.

The King went up to him and said: "I have come to you, wise hermit, to ask you to answer three questions: How can I learn to do the right thing at the right time? Who are the people I most need, and to whom should I, therefore, pay more attention than to the rest? And, what affairs are the most important, and need my first attention?"

The hermit listened to the King, but answered nothing. He just spat on his hand and recommenced digging.

"You are tired," said the King, "let me take the spade and work awhile for you."

"Thanks!" said the hermit, and, giving the spade to the King, he sat down on the ground.

When he had dug two beds, the King stopped and repeated his questions. The hermit again gave no answer, but rose, stretched out his hand for the spade, and said:

"Now rest awhile-and let me work a bit."

But the King did not give him the spade, and continued to dig. One hour passed, and another. The sun began to sink behind the trees, and the King at last stuck the spade into the ground, and said:

"I came to you, wise man, for an answer to my questions. If you can give me none, tell me so, and I will return home."

"Here comes some one running," said the hermit, "let us see who it is."

The King turned round, and saw a bearded man come running out of the wood. The man held his hands pressed against his stomach, and blood was flowing from under them. When he reached the King, he fell fainting on the ground moaning feebly. The King and the hermit unfastened the man's clothing. There was a large wound in his stomach. The King washed it as best he could, and bandaged it with his handkerchief and with a towel the hermit had. But the blood would not stop flowing, and the King again and again removed the bandage soaked with warm blood, and washed and rebandaged the wound. When at last the blood ceased flowing, the man revived and asked for something to drink. The King brought fresh water and gave it to him. Meanwhile the sun had set, and it had become cool. So the King, with the hermit's help, carried the wounded man into the hut and laid him on the bed. Lying on the bed the man closed his eyes and was quiet; but the King was so tired with his walk and with the work he had done, that he crouched down on the threshold, and also fell asleep—so soundly that he slept all through the short summer night. When he awoke in the morning, it was long before he could remember where he was, or who was the strange bearded man lying on the bed and gazing intently at him with shining eyes.

"Forgive me!" said the bearded man in a weak voice, when he saw that the King was awake and was looking at him.

"I do not know you, and have nothing to forgive you for," said the King.

"You do not know me, but I know you. I am that enemy of yours who swore to revenge himself on you, because you executed his brother and seized his property. I knew you had gone alone to see the hermit, and I resolved to kill you on your way back. But the day passed and you did not return. So I came out from my ambush to find you, and I came upon your bodyguard, and they recognized me, and wounded me. I escaped from them, but should have bled to death had you not dressed my wound. I wished to kill you, and you have saved my life. Now, if I live, and if you wish it, I will serve you as your most faithful slave, and will bid my sons do the same. Forgive me!"

The King was very glad to have made peace with his enemy so easily, and to have gained him for a friend, and he not only forgave him, but said he would send his servants and his own physician to attend him, and promised to restore his property.

Having taken leave of the wounded man, the King went out into the porch and looked around for the hermit. Before going away he wished once more to beg an answer to the questions he had put. The hermit was outside, on his knees, sowing seeds in the beds that had been dug the day before.

The King approached him, and said:

"For the last time, I pray you to answer my questions, wise man."

"You have already been answered!" said the hermit, still crouching on his thin legs, and looking up at the King, who stood before him.

"How answered? What do you mean?" asked the King.

"Do you not see," replied the hermit. "If you had not pitied my weakness yesterday, and had not dug those beds for me, but had gone your way, that man would have attacked you, and you would have repented of not having stayed with me. So the most important time was when you were digging the beds; and I was the most important man; and to do me good was your most important business. Afterwards when that man ran to us, the most important time was when you were attending to him, for if you had not bound up his wounds he would have died without having made peace with you. So he was the most important man, and what you did for him was your most important business. Remember then: there is only one time that is important—Now! It is the most important time because it is the only time when we have any power. The most necessary man is he with whom you are, for no man knows whether he will ever have dealings with anyone else: and the most important affair is, to do him good, because for that purpose alone was man sent into this life!"

THE COFFEE-HOUSE OF SURAT
(After Bernardin de Saint-Pierre)

In the town of Surat, in India, was a coffee-house where many travellers and foreigners from all parts of the world met and conversed.

One day a learned Persian theologian visited this coffee-house. He was a man who had spent his life studying the nature of the Deity, and reading and writing books upon the subject. He had thought, read, and written so much about God, that eventually he lost his wits, became quite confused, and ceased even to believe in the existence of a God. The Shah, hearing of this, had banished him from Persia.

After having argued all his life about the First Cause, this unfortunate theologian had ended by quite perplexing himself, and instead of understanding that he had lost his own reason, he began to think that there was no higher Reason controlling the universe.

This man had an African slave who followed him everywhere. When the theologian entered the coffee-house, the slave remained outside, near the door, sitting on a stone in the glare of the sun, and driving away the flies that buzzed around him. The Persian having settled down on a divan in the coffee-house, ordered himself a cup of opium. When he had drunk it and the opium had begun to quicken the workings of his brain, he addressed his slave through the open door:

"Tell me, wretched slave," said he, "do you think there is a God, or not?"

"Of course there is," said the slave, and immediately drew from under his girdle a small idol of wood.

"There," said he, "that is the God who has guarded me from the day of my birth. Every one in our country worships the fetish tree, from the wood of which this God was made."

This conversation between the theologian and his slave was listened to with surprise by the other guests in the coffee-house. They were astonished at the master's question, and yet more so at the slave's reply.

One of them, a Brahmin, on hearing the words spoken by the slave, turned to him and said:

"Miserable fool! Is it possible you believe that God can be carried under a man's girdle? There is one God—Brahma, and he is greater than the whole world, for he created it. Brahma is the One, the mighty God, and in His honour are built the temples on the Ganges' banks, where his true priests, the Brahmins, worship him. They know the true God, and none but they. A thousand score of years have passed, and yet through revolution after revolution these priests have held their sway, because Brahma, the one true God, has protected them."

So spoke the Brahmin, thinking to convince everyone; but a Jewish broker who was present replied to him, and said:

"No! the temple of the true God is not in India. Neither does God protect the Brahmin caste. The true God is not the God of the Brahmins, but of Abraham, Isaac, and Jacob. None does He protect but His chosen people, the Israelites. From the commencement of the world, our nation has been beloved of Him, and ours alone. If we are now scattered over the whole earth, it is but to try us; for God has promised that He will one day gather His people together in Jerusalem. Then, with the Temple of Jerusalem—the wonder of the ancient world—restored to its splendor, shall Israel be established a ruler over all nations."

So spoke the Jew, and burst into tears. He wished to say more, but an Italian missionary who was there interrupted him.

"What you are saying is untrue," said he to the Jew. "You attribute injustice to God. He cannot love your nation above the rest. Nay rather, even if it be true that of old He favored the Israelites, it is now nineteen hundred years since they angered Him, and caused Him to destroy their nation and scatter them over the earth, so that their faith makes no converts and has died out except here and there. God shows preference to no nation, but calls all who wish to be saved to the bosom of the Catholic Church of Rome, the one outside whose borders no salvation can be found."

So spoke the Italian. But a Protestant minister, who happened to be present, growing pale, turned to the Catholic missionary and exclaimed:

"How can you say that salvation belongs to your religion? Those only will be saved, who serve God according to the Gospel, in spirit and in truth, as bidden by the word of Christ."

Then a Turk, an office-holder in the custom-house at Surat, who was sitting in the coffee-house smoking a pipe, turned with an air of superiority to both the Christians.

"Your belief in your Roman religion is vain," said he. "It was superseded twelve hundred years ago by the true faith: that of Mohammed! You cannot but observe how the true Mohammed faith continues to spread both in Europe and Asia, and even in the enlightened country of China. You say yourselves that God has rejected the Jews; and, as a proof, you quote the fact that the Jews are humiliated and their faith does not spread. Confess then the truth of Mohammedanism, for it is triumphant and spreads far and wide. None will be saved but the followers of Mohammed, God's latest prophet; and of them, only the followers of Omar, and not of Ali, for the latter are false to the faith."

To this the Persian theologian, who was of the sect of Ali, wished to reply; but by this time a great dispute had arisen among all the strangers of different faiths and creeds present. There were Abyssinian Christians, Llamas from Thibet, Ismailians and Fireworshippers. They all argued about the nature of God, and how He should be worshipped. Each of them asserted that in his country alone was the true God known and rightly worshipped.

Every one argued and shouted, except a Chinaman, a student of Confucius, who sat quietly in one corner of the coffee-house, not joining in the dispute. He sat there drinking tea and listening to what the others said, but did not speak himself.

The Turk noticed him sitting there, and appealed to him, saying:

"You can confirm what I say, my good Chinaman. You hold your peace, but if you spoke I know you would uphold my opinion. Traders from your country, who come to me for assistance, tell me that though many religions have been introduced into China, you Chinese consider Mohammedanism the best of all, and adopt it willingly. Confirm, then, my words, and tell us your opinion of the true God and of His prophet."

"Yes, yes," said the rest, turning to the Chinaman, "let us hear what you think on the subject."

The Chinaman, the student of Confucius, closed his eyes, and thought a while. Then he opened them again, and drawing his hands out of the wide sleeves of his garment, and folding them on his breast, he spoke as follows, in a calm and quiet voice.

Sirs, it seems to me that it is chiefly pride that prevents men agreeing with one another on matters of faith. If you care to listen to me, I will tell you a story which will explain this by an example.

I came here from China on an English steamer which had been round the world. We stopped for fresh water, and landed on the east coast of the island of Sumatra. It was midday, and some of us, having landed, sat in the shade of some cocoanut palms by the seashore, not far from a native village. We were a party of men of different nationalities.

As we sat there, a blind man approached us. We learned afterwards that he had gone blind from gazing too long and too persistently at the sun, trying to find out what it is, in order to seize its light.

He strove a long time to accomplish this, constantly looking at the sun; but the only result was that his eyes were injured by its brightness, and he became blind.

Then he said to himself:

"The light of the sun is not a liquid; for if it were a liquid it would be possible to pour it from one vessel into another, and it would be moved, like water, by the wind. Neither is it fire; for if it were fire, water would extinguish it. Neither is light a spirit, for it is seen by the eye; nor is it matter, for it cannot be moved. Therefore, as the light of the sun is neither liquid, nor fire, nor spirit, nor matter, it is—nothing!"

So he argued, and, as a result of always looking at the sun and always thinking about it, he lost both his sight and his reason. And when he went quite blind, he became fully convinced that the sun did not exist.

With this blind man came a slave, who after placing his master in the shade of a cocoanut tree, picked up a cocoanut from the ground, and began making it into a night-light. He twisted a wick from the fibre of the cocoanut: squeezed oil from the nut in the shell, and soaked the wick in it.

As the slave sat doing this, the blind man sighed and said to him:

"Well, slave, was I not right when I told you there is no sun? Do you not see how dark it is? Yet people say there is a sun.... But if so, what is it?"

"I do not know what the sun is," said the slave. "That is no business of mine. But I know what light is. Here I have made a night-light, by the help of which I can serve you and find anything I want in the hut."

And the slave picked up the cocoanut shell, saying:

"This is my sun."

A lame man with crutches, who was sitting near by, heard these words, and laughed:

"You have evidently been blind all your life," said he to the blind man, "not to know what the sun is. I will tell you what it is. The sun is a ball of fire, which rises every morning out of the sea and goes down again among the mountains of our island each evening. We have all seen this, and if you had had your eyesight you too would have seen it."

A fisherman, who had been listening to the conversation said:

"It is plain enough that you have never been beyond your own island. If you were not lame, and if you had been out as I have in a fishing-boat, you would know that the sun does not set among the mountains of our island, but as it rises from the ocean every morning so it sets again in the sea every night. What I am telling you is true, for I see it every day with my own eyes."

Then an Indian who was of our party, interrupted him by saying:

"I am astonished that a reasonable man should talk such nonsense. How can a ball of fire possibly descend into the water and not be extinguished? The sun is not a ball of fire at all, it is the Deity named Deva, who rides for ever in a chariot round the golden mountain, Meru. Sometimes the evil serpents Ragu and Ketu attack Deva and swallow him: and then the earth is dark. But our priests pray that the Deity may be released, and then he is set free. Only such ignorant men as you, who have never been beyond their own island, can imagine that the sun shines for their country alone."

Then the master of an Egyptian vessel, who was present, spoke in his turn.

"No," said he, "you also are wrong. The sun is not a Deity, and does not move only round India and its golden mountain. I have sailed much on the Black Sea, and along the coasts of Arabia, and have been to Madagascar and to the Philippines. The sun lights the whole earth, and not India alone. It does not circle round one mountain, but rises far in the East, beyond the Isles of Japan, and sets far, far away in the West, beyond the islands of England. That is why the Japanese call their country 'Nippon,' that is, 'the birth of the sun.' I know this well, for I have myself seen much, and heard more from my grandfather, who sailed to the very ends of the sea."

He would have gone on, but an English sailor from our ship interrupted him.

"There is no country," he said "where people know so much about the sun's movements as in England. The sun, as every one in England knows, rises nowhere and sets nowhere. It is always moving round the earth. We can be sure of this for we have just been round the world ourselves, and nowhere knocked up against the sun. Wherever we went, the sun showed itself in the morning and hid itself at night, just as it does here."

And the Englishman took a stick and, drawing circles on the sand, tried to explain how the sun moves in the heavens and goes round the world. But he was unable to explain it clearly, and pointing to the ship's pilot said:

"This man knows more about it than I do. He can explain it properly."

The pilot, who was an intelligent man, had listened in silence to the talk till he was asked to speak. Now every one turned to him, and he said:

"You are all misleading one another, and are yourselves deceived. The sun does not go round the earth, but the earth goes round the sun, revolving as it goes, and turning towards the sun in the course of each twenty-four hours, not only Japan, and the Philippines, and Sumatra where we now are, but Africa, and Europe, and America, and many lands besides. The sun does not shine for some one mountain, or for some one island, or for some one sea, nor even for one earth alone, but for other planets as well as our earth. If you would only look up at the heavens, instead of at the ground beneath your own feet, you might all understand this, and would then no longer suppose that the sun shines for you, or for your country alone."

Thus spoke the wise pilot, who had voyaged much about the world, and had gazed much upon the heavens above.

"So on matters of faith," continued the Chinaman, the student of Confucius, "it is pride that causes error and discord among men. As with the sun, so it is with God. Each man wants to have a special God of his own, or at least a special God for his native land. Each nation wishes to confine in its own temples Him, whom the world cannot contain.

"Can any temple compare with that which God Himself has built to unite all men in one faith and one religion?

"All human temples are built on the model of this temple, which is God's own world. Every temple has its fonts, its vaulted roof, its lamps, its pictures or sculptures, its inscriptions, its books of the law, its offerings, its altars and its priests. But in what temple is there such a font as the ocean; such a vault as that of the heavens; such lamps as the sun, moon, and stars; or any figures to be compared with living, loving, mutually-helpful men? Where are there any records of God's goodness so easy to understand as the blessings which God has strewn abroad for man's happiness? Where is there any book of the law so clear to each man as that written in his heart? What sacrifices equal the self-denials which loving men and women make for one another? And what altar can be compared with the heart of a good man, on which God Himself accepts the sacrifice?

"The higher a man's conception of God, the better will he know Him. And the better he knows God, the nearer will he draw to Him, imitating His goodness, His mercy, and His love of man.

"Therefore, let him who sees the sun's whole light filling the world, refrain from blaming or despising the superstitious man, who in his own idol sees one ray of that same light. Let him not despise even the unbeliever who is blind and cannot see the sun at all."

So spoke the Chinaman, the student of Confucius; and all who were present in the coffee-house were silent, and disputed no more as to whose faith was the best.

HOW MUCH LAND DOES A MAN NEED?
I

An elder sister came to visit her younger sister in the country. The elder was married to a tradesman in town, the younger to a peasant in the village. As the sisters sat over their tea talking, the elder began to boast of the advantages of town life: saying how comfortably they lived there, how well they dressed, what fine clothes her children wore, what good things they ate and drank, and how she went to the theatre, promenades, and entertainments.

The younger sister was piqued, and in turn disparaged the life of a tradesman, and stood up for that of a peasant.

"I would not change my way of life for yours," said she. "We may live roughly, but at least we are free from anxiety. You live in better style than we do, but though you often earn more than you need, you are very likely to lose all you have. You know the proverb, 'Loss and gain are brothers twain.' It often happens that people who are wealthy one day are begging their bread the next. Our way is safer. Though a peasant's life is not a fat one, it is a long one. We shall never grow rich, but we shall always have enough to eat."

The elder sister said sneeringly:

"Enough? Yes, if you like to share with the pigs and the calves! What do you know of elegance or manners! However much your good man may slave, you will die as you are living-on a dung heap-and your children the same."

"Well, what of that?" replied the younger. "Of course our work is rough and coarse. But, on the other hand, it is sure; and we need not bow to any one. But you, in your towns, are surrounded by temptations; today all may be right, but tomorrow the Evil One may tempt your husband with cards, wine, or women, and all will go to ruin. Don't such things happen often enough?"

Pahom, the master of the house, was lying on the top of the oven, and he listened to the women's chatter.

"It is perfectly true," thought he. "Busy as we are from childhood tilling Mother Earth, we peasants have no time to let any nonsense settle in our heads. Our only trouble is that we haven't land enough. If I had plenty of land, I shouldn't fear the Devil himself!"

The women finished their tea, chatted a while about dress, and then cleared away the tea-things and lay down to sleep.

But the Devil had been sitting behind the oven, and had heard all that was said. He was pleased that the peasant's wife had led her husband into boasting, and that he had said that if he had plenty of land he would not fear the Devil himself.

"All right," thought the Devil. "We will have a tussle. I'll give you land enough; and by means of that land I will get you into my power."

II

Close to the village there lived a lady, a small landowner, who had an estate of about three hundred acres. She had always lived on good terms with the peasants, until she engaged as her steward an old soldier, who took to burdening the people with fines. However careful Pahom tried to be, it happened again and again that now a horse of his got among the lady's oats, now a cow strayed into her garden, now his calves found their way into her meadows-and he always had to pay a fine.

Pahom paid, but grumbled, and, going home in a temper, was rough with his family. All through that summer Pahom had much trouble because of this steward; and he was even glad when winter came and the cattle had to be stabled. Though he grudged the fodder when they could no longer graze on the pasture-land, at least he was free from anxiety about them.

In the winter the news got about that the lady was going to sell her land, and that the keeper of the inn on the high road was bargaining for it. When the peasants heard this they were very much alarmed.

"Well," thought they, "if the innkeeper gets the land he will worry us with fines worse than the lady's steward. We all depend on that estate."

So the peasants went on behalf of their Commune, and asked the lady not to sell the land to the innkeeper; offering her a better price for it themselves. The lady agreed to let them have it. Then the peasants tried to arrange for the Commune to buy the whole estate, so that it might be held by all in common. They met twice to discuss it, but could not settle the matter; the Evil One sowed discord among them, and they could not agree. So they decided to buy the land individually, each according to his means; and the lady agreed to this plan as she had to the other.

Presently Pahom heard that a neighbor of his was buying fifty acres, and that the lady had consented to accept one half in cash and to wait a year for the other half. Pahom felt envious.

"Look at that," thought he, "the land is all being sold, and I shall get none of it." So he spoke to his wife.

"Other people are buying," said he, "and we must also buy twenty acres or so. Life is becoming impossible. That steward is simply crushing us with his fines."

So they put their heads together and considered how they could manage to buy it. They had one hundred roubles laid by. They sold a colt, and one half of their bees; hired out one of their sons as a laborer, and took his wages in advance; borrowed the rest from a brother-in-law, and so scraped together half the purchase money.

Having done this, Pahom chose out a farm of forty acres, some of it wooded, and went to the lady to bargain for it. They came to an agreement, and he shook hands with her upon it, and paid her a deposit in advance. Then they went to town and signed the deeds; he paying half the price down, and undertaking to pay the remainder within two years.

So now Pahom had land of his own. He borrowed seed, and sowed it on the land he had bought. The harvest was a good one, and within a year he had managed to pay off his debts both to the lady and to his brother-in-law. So he became a landowner, ploughing and sowing his own land, making hay on his own land, cutting his own trees, and feeding his cattle on his own pasture. When he went out to plough his fields, or to look at his growing corn, or at his grass meadows, his heart would fill with joy. The grass that grew and the flowers that bloomed there, seemed to him unlike any that grew elsewhere. Formerly, when he had passed by that land, it had appeared the same as any other land, but now it seemed quite different.

III

So Pahom was well contented, and everything would have been right if the neighboring peasants would only not have trespassed on his corn-fields and meadows. He appealed to them most civilly, but they still went on: now the Communal herdsmen would let the village cows stray into his meadows; then horses from the night pasture would get among his corn. Pahom turned them out again and again, and forgave their owners, and for a long time he forbore from prosecuting any one. But at last he lost patience and complained to the District Court. He knew it was the peasants' want of land, and no evil intent on their part, that caused the trouble; but he thought:

"I cannot go on overlooking it, or they will destroy all I have. They must be taught a lesson."

So he had them up, gave them one lesson, and then another, and two or three of the peasants were fined. After a time Pahom's neighbours began to bear him a grudge for this, and would now and then let their cattle on his land on purpose. One peasant even got into Pahom's wood at night and cut down five young lime trees for their bark. Pahom passing through the wood one day noticed something white. He came nearer, and saw the stripped trunks lying on the ground, and close by stood the stumps, where the tree had been. Pahom was furious.

"If he had only cut one here and there it would have been bad enough," thought Pahom, "but the rascal has actually cut down a whole clump. If I could only find out who did this, I would pay him out."

He racked his brains as to who it could be. Finally he decided: "It must be Simon-no one else could have done it." Se he went to Simon's homestead to have a look around, but he found nothing, and only had an angry scene. However' he now felt more certain than ever that Simon had done it, and he lodged a complaint. Simon was summoned. The case was tried, and re-tried, and at the end of it all Simon was acquitted, there being no evidence against him. Pahom felt still more aggrieved, and let his anger loose upon the Elder and the Judges.

"You let thieves grease your palms," said he. "If you were honest folk yourselves, you would not let a thief go free."

So Pahom quarrelled with the Judges and with his neighbors. Threats to burn his building began to be uttered. So though Pahom had more land, his place in the Commune was much worse than before.

About this time a rumor got about that many people were moving to new parts.

"There's no need for me to leave my land," thought Pahom. "But some of the others might leave our village, and then there would be more room for us. I would take over their land myself, and make my estate a bit bigger. I could then live more at ease. As it is, I am still too cramped to be comfortable."

One day Pahom was sitting at home, when a peasant passing through the village, happened to call in. He was allowed to stay the night, and supper was given him. Pahom had a talk with this peasant and asked him where he came from. The stranger answered that he came from beyond the Volga, where he had been working. One word led to another, and the man went on to say that many people were settling in those parts. He told how some people from his village had settled there. They had joined the Commune, and had had twenty-five acres per man granted them. The land was so good, he said, that the rye sown on it grew as high as a horse, and so thick that five cuts of a sickle made a sheaf. One peasant, he said, had brought nothing with him but his bare hands, and now he had six horses and two cows of his own.

Pahom's heart kindled with desire. He thought:

"Why should I suffer in this narrow hole, if one can live so well elsewhere? I will sell my land and my homestead here, and with the money I will start afresh over there and get everything new. In this crowded place one is always having trouble. But I must first go and find out all about it myself."

Towards summer he got ready and started. He went down the Volga on a steamer to Samara, then walked another three hundred miles on foot, and at last reached the place. It was just as the stranger had said. The peasants had plenty of land: every man had twenty-five acres of Communal land given him for his use, and any one who had money could buy, besides, at fifty-cents an acre as much good freehold land as he wanted.

Having found out all he wished to know, Pahom returned home as autumn came on, and began selling off his belongings. He sold his land at a profit, sold his homestead and all his cattle, and withdrew from membership of the Commune. He only waited till the spring, and then started with his family for the new settlement.

IV

As soon as Pahom and his family arrived at their new abode, he applied for admission into the Commune of a large village. He stood treat to the Elders, and obtained the necessary documents. Five shares of Communal land were given him for his own and his sons' use: that is to say—125 acres (not altogether, but in different fields) besides the use of the Communal pasture. Pahom put up the buildings he needed, and bought cattle. Of the Communal land alone he had three times as much as at his former home, and the land was good corn-land. He was ten times better off than he had been. He had plenty of arable land and pasturage, and could keep as many head of cattle as he liked.

At first, in the bustle of building and settling down, Pahom was pleased with it all, but when he got used to it he began to think that even here he had not enough land. The first year, he sowed wheat on his share of the Communal land, and had a good crop. He wanted to go on sowing wheat, but had not enough Communal land for the purpose, and what he had already used was not available; for in those parts wheat is only sown on virgin soil or on fallow land. It is sown for one or two years, and then the land lies fallow till it is again overgrown with prairie grass. There were many who wanted such land, and there was not enough for all; so that people quarrelled about it. Those who were better off, wanted it for growing wheat, and those who were poor, wanted it to let to dealers, so that they might raise money to pay their taxes. Pahom wanted to sow more wheat; so he rented land from a dealer for a year. He sowed much wheat and had a fine crop, but the land was too far from the village—the wheat had to be carted more than ten miles. After a time Pahom noticed that some peasant-dealers were living on separate farms, and were growing wealthy; and he thought:

"If I were to buy some freehold land, and have a homestead on it, it would be a different thing, altogether. Then it would all be nice and compact."

The question of buying freehold land recurred to him again and again.

He went on in the same way for three years; renting land and sowing wheat. The seasons turned out well and the crops were good, so that he began to lay money by. He might have gone on living contentedly, but he grew tired of having to rent other people's land every year, and having to scramble for it. Wherever there was good land to be had, the peasants would rush for it and it was taken up at once, so that unless you were sharp about it you got none. It happened in the third year that he and a dealer together rented a piece of pasture land from some peasants; and they had already ploughed it up, when there was some dispute, and the peasants went to law about it, and things fell out so that the labor was all lost. "If it were my own land," thought Pahom, "I should be independent, and there would not be all this unpleasantness."

So Pahom began looking out for land which he could buy; and he came across a peasant who had bought thirteen hundred acres, but having got into difficulties was willing to sell again cheap. Pahom bargained and haggled with him, and at last they settled the price at 1,500 roubles, part in cash and part to be paid later. They had all but clinched the matter, when a passing dealer happened to stop at Pahom's one day to get a feed for his horse. He drank tea with Pahom, and they had a talk. The dealer said that he was just returning from the land of the Bashkirs, far away, where he had bought thirteen thousand acres of land all for 1,000 roubles. Pahom questioned him further, and the tradesman said:

"All one need do is to make friends with the chiefs. I gave away about one hundred roubles' worth of dressing-gowns and carpets, besides a case of tea, and I gave wine to those who would drink it; and I got the land for less than two cents an acre. And he showed Pahom the title-deeds, saying:

"The land lies near a river, and the whole prairie is virgin soil."

Pahom plied him with questions, and the tradesman said:

"There is more land there than you could cover if you walked a year, and it all belongs to the Bashkirs. They are as simple as sheep, and land can be got almost for nothing."

"There now," thought Pahom, "with my one thousand roubles, why should I get only thirteen hundred acres, and saddle myself with a debt besides. If I take it out there, I can get more than ten times as much for the money."

V

Pahom inquired how to get to the place, and as soon as the tradesman had left him, he prepared to go there himself. He left his wife to look after the homestead, and started on his journey taking his man with him. They stopped at a town on their way, and bought a case of tea, some wine, and other presents, as the tradesman had advised. On and on they went until they had gone more than three hundred miles, and on the seventh day they came to a place where the Bashkirs had pitched their tents. It was all just as the tradesman had said. The people lived on the steppes, by a river, in felt-covered tents. They neither tilled the ground, nor ate bread. Their cattle and horses grazed in herds on the steppe. The colts were tethered behind the tents, and the mares were driven to them twice a day. The mares were milked, and from the milk kumiss was made. It was the women who prepared kumiss, and they also made cheese. As far as the men were concerned, drinking kumiss and tea, eating mutton, and playing on their pipes, was all they cared about. They were all stout and merry, and all the summer long they never thought of doing any work. They were quite ignorant, and knew no Russian, but were good-natured enough.

As soon as they saw Pahom, they came out of their tents and gathered round their visitor. An interpreter was found, and Pahom told them he had come about some land. The Bashkirs seemed very glad; they took Pahom and led him into one of the best tents, where they made him sit on some down cushions placed on a carpet, while they sat round him. They gave him tea and kumiss, and had a sheep killed, and gave him mutton to eat. Pahom took presents out of his cart and distributed them among the Bashkirs, and divided amongst them the tea. The Bashkirs were delighted. They talked a great deal among themselves, and then told the interpreter to translate.

"They wish to tell you," said the interpreter, "that they like you, and that it is our custom to do all we can to please a guest and to repay him for his gifts. You have given us presents, now tell us which of the things we possess please you best, that we may present them to you."

"What pleases me best here," answered Pahom, "is your land. Our land is crowded, and the soil is exhausted; but you have plenty of land and it is good land. I never saw the like of it."

The interpreter translated. The Bashkirs talked among themselves for a while. Pahom could not understand what they were saying, but saw that they were much amused, and that they shouted and laughed. Then they were silent and looked at Pahom while the interpreter said:

"They wish me to tell you that in return for your presents they will gladly give you as much land as you want. You have only to point it out with your hand and it is yours."

The Bashkirs talked again for a while and began to dispute. Pahom asked what they were disputing about, and the interpreter told him that some of them thought they ought to ask their Chief about the land and not act in his absence, while others thought there was no need to wait for his return.

VI

While the Bashkirs were disputing, a man in a large fox-fur cap appeared on the scene. They all became silent and rose to their feet. The interpreter said, "This is our Chief himself."

Pahom immediately fetched the best dressing-gown and five pounds of tea, and offered these to the Chief. The Chief accepted them, and seated himself in the place of honour. The Bashkirs at once began telling him something. The Chief listened for a while, then made a sign with his head for them to be silent, and addressing himself to Pahom, said in Russian:

"Well, let it be so. Choose whatever piece of land you like; we have plenty of it."

"How can I take as much as I like?" thought Pahom. "I must get a deed to make it secure, or else they may say, 'It is yours,' and afterwards may take it away again."

"Thank you for your kind words," he said aloud. "You have much land, and I only want a little. But I should like to be sure which bit is mine. Could it not be measured and made over to me? Life and death are in God's hands. You good people give it to me, but your children might wish to take it away again."

"You are quite right," said the Chief. "We will make it over to you."

"I heard that a dealer had been here," continued Pahom, "and that you gave him a little land, too, and signed title-deeds to that effect. I should like to have it done in the same way."

The Chief understood.

"Yes," replied he, "that can be done quite easily. We have a scribe, and we will go to town with you and have the deed properly sealed."

"And what will be the price?" asked Pahom.

"Our price is always the same: one thousand roubles a day."

Pahom did not understand.

"A day? What measure is that? How many acres would that be?"

"We do not know how to reckon it out," said the Chief. "We sell it by the day. As much as you can go round on your feet in a day is yours, and the price is one thousand roubles a day."

Pahom was surprised.

"But in a day you can get round a large tract of land," he said.

The Chief laughed.

"It will all be yours!" said he. "But there is one condition: If you don't return on the same day to the spot whence you started, your money is lost."

"But how am I to mark the way that I have gone?"

"Why, we shall go to any spot you like, and stay there. You must start from that spot and make your round, taking a spade with you. Wherever you think necessary, make a mark. At every turning, dig a hole and pile up the turf; then afterwards we will go round with a plough from hole to hole. You may make as large a circuit as you please, but before the sun sets you must return to the place you started from. All the land you cover will be yours."

Pahom was delighted. It-was decided to start early next morning. They talked a while, and after drinking some more kumiss and eating some more mutton, they had tea again, and then the night came on. They gave Pahom a feather-bed to sleep on, and the Bashkirs dispersed for the night, promising to assemble the next morning at daybreak and ride out before sunrise to the appointed spot.

VII

Pahom lay on the feather-bed, but could not sleep. He kept thinking about the land.

"What a large tract I will mark off!" thought he. "I can easily go thirty-five miles in a day. The days are long now, and within a circuit of thirty-five miles what a lot of land there will be! I will sell the poorer land, or let it to peasants, but I'll pick out the best and farm it. I will buy two ox-teams, and hire two more laborers. About a hundred and fifty acres shall be plough-land, and I will pasture cattle on the rest."

Pahom lay awake all night, and dozed off only just before dawn. Hardly were his eyes closed when he had a dream. He thought he was lying in that same tent, and heard somebody chuckling outside. He wondered who it could be, and rose and went out, and he saw the Bashkir Chief sitting in front of the tent holding his side and rolling about with laughter. Going nearer to the Chief, Pahom asked: "What are you laughing at?" But he saw that it was no longer the Chief, but the dealer who had recently stopped at his house and had told him about the land. Just as Pahom was going to ask, "Have you been here long?" he saw that it was not the dealer, but the peasant who had come up from the Volga, long ago, to Pahom's old home. Then he saw that it was not the peasant either, but the Devil himself with hoofs and horns, sitting there and chuckling, and before him lay a man barefoot, prostrate on the ground, with only trousers and a shirt on. And Pahom dreamt that he looked more attentively to see what sort of a man it was lying there, and he saw that the man was dead, and that it was himself! He awoke horror-struck.

"What things one does dream," thought he.

Looking round he saw through the open door that the dawn was breaking.

"It's time to wake them up," thought he. "We ought to be starting."

He got up, roused his man (who was sleeping in his cart), bade him harness; and went to call the Bashkirs.

"It's time to go to the steppe to measure the land," he said.

The Bashkirs rose and assembled, and the Chief came, too. Then they began drinking kumiss again, and offered Pahom some tea, but he would not wait.

"If we are to go, let us go. It is high time," said he.

VIII

The Bashkirs got ready and they all started: some mounted on horses, and some in carts. Pahom drove in his own small cart with his servant, and took a spade with him. When they reached the steppe, the morning red was beginning to kindle. They ascended a hillock (called by the Bashkirs a shikhan) and dismounting from their carts and their horses, gathered in one spot. The Chief came up to Pahom and stretched out his arm towards the plain:

"See," said he, "all this, as far as your eye can reach, is ours. You may have any part of it you like."

Pahom's eyes glistened: it was all virgin soil, as flat as the palm of your hand, as black as the seed of a poppy, and in the hollows different kinds of grasses grew breast high.

The Chief took off his fox-fur cap, placed it on the ground and said:

"This will be the mark. Start from here, and return here again. All the land you go round shall be yours."

Pahom took out his money and put it on the cap. Then he took off his outer coat, remaining in his sleeveless under coat. He unfastened his girdle and tied it tight below his stomach, put a little bag of bread into the breast of his coat, and tying a flask of water to his girdle, he drew up the tops of his boots, took the spade from his man, and stood ready to start. He considered for some moments which way he had better go—it was tempting everywhere.

"No matter," he concluded, "I will go towards the rising sun."

He turned his face to the east, stretched himself, and waited for the sun to appear above the rim.

"I must lose no time," he thought, "and it is easier walking while it is still cool."

The sun's rays had hardly flashed above the horizon, before Pahom, carrying the spade over his shoulder, went down into the steppe.

Pahom started walking neither slowly nor quickly. After having gone a thousand yards he stopped, dug a hole and placed pieces of turf one on another to make it more visible. Then he went on; and now that he had walked off his stiffness he quickened his pace. After a while he dug another hole.

Pahom looked back. The hillock could be distinctly seen in the sunlight, with the people on it, and the glittering tires of the cartwheels. At a rough guess Pahom concluded that he had walked three miles. It was growing warmer; he took off his under-coat, flung it across his shoulder, and went on again. It had grown quite warm now; he looked at the sun, it was time to think of breakfast.

"The first shift is done, but there are four in a day, and it is too soon yet to turn. But I will just take off my boots," said he to himself.

He sat down, took off his boots, stuck them into his girdle, and went on. It was easy walking now.

"I will go on for another three miles," thought he, "and then turn to the left. The spot is so fine, that it would be a pity to lose it. The further one goes, the better the land seems."

He went straight on a for a while, and when he looked round, the hillock was scarcely visible and the people on it looked like black ants, and he could just see something glistening there in the sun.

"Ah," thought Pahom, "I have gone far enough in this direction, it is time to turn. Besides I am in a regular sweat, and very thirsty."

He stopped, dug a large hole, and heaped up pieces of turf. Next he untied his flask, had a drink, and then turned sharply to the left. He went on and on; the grass was high, and it was very hot.

Pahom began to grow tired: he looked at the sun and saw that it was noon.

"Well," he thought, "I must have a rest."

He sat down, and ate some bread and drank some water; but he did not lie down, thinking that if he did he might fall asleep. After sitting a little while, he went on again. At first he walked easily: the food had strengthened him; but it had become terribly hot, and he felt sleepy; still he went on, thinking: "An hour to suffer, a life-time to live."

He went a long way in this direction also, and was about to turn to the left again, when he perceived a damp hollow: "It would be a pity to leave that out," he thought. "Flax would do well there." So he went on past the hollow, and dug a hole on the other side of it before he turned the corner. Pahom looked towards the hillock. The heat made the air hazy: it seemed to be quivering, and through the haze the people on the hillock could scarcely be seen.

"Ah!" thought Pahom, "I have made the sides too long; I must make this one shorter." And he went along the third side, stepping faster. He looked at the sun: it was nearly half way to the horizon, and he had not yet done two miles of the third side of the square. He was still ten miles from the goal.

"No," he thought, "though it will make my land lopsided, I must hurry back in a straight line now. I might go too far, and as it is I have a great deal of land."

So Pahom hurriedly dug a hole, and turned straight towards the hillock.

IX

Pahom went straight towards the hillock, but he now walked with difficulty. He was done up with the heat, his bare feet were cut and bruised, and his legs began to fail. He longed to rest, but it was impossible if he meant to get back before sunset. The sun waits for no man, and it was sinking lower and lower.

"Oh dear," he thought, "if only I have not blundered trying for too much! What if I am too late?"

He looked towards the hillock and at the sun. He was still far from his goal, and the sun was already near the rim. Pahom walked on and on; it was very hard walking, but he went quicker and quicker. He pressed on, but was still far from the place. He began running, threw away his coat, his boots, his flask, and his cap, and kept only the spade which he used as a support.

"What shall I do," he thought again, "I have grasped too much, and ruined the whole affair. I can't get there before the sun sets."

And this fear made him still more breathless. Pahom went on running, his soaking shirt and trousers stuck to him, and his mouth was parched. His breast was working like a blacksmith's bellows, his heart was beating like a hammer, and his legs were giving way as if they did not belong to him. Pahom was seized with terror lest he should die of the strain.

Though afraid of death, he could not stop. "After having run all that way they will call me a fool if I stop now," thought he. And he ran on and on, and drew near and heard the Bashkirs yelling and shouting to him, and their cries inflamed his heart still more. He gathered his last strength and ran on.

The sun was close to the rim, and cloaked in mist looked large, and red as blood. Now, yes now, it was about to set! The sun was quite low, but he was also quite near his aim. Pahom could already see the people on the hillock waving their arms to hurry him up. He could see the fox-fur cap on the ground, and the money on it, and the Chief sitting on the ground holding his sides. And Pahom remembered his dream.

"There is plenty of land," thought he, "but will God let me live on it? I have lost my life, I have lost my life! I shall never reach that spot!"

Pahom looked at the sun, which had reached the earth: one side of it had already disappeared. With all his remaining strength he rushed on, bending his body forward so that his legs could hardly follow fast enough to keep him from falling. Just as he reached the hillock it suddenly grew dark. He looked up—the sun had already set. He gave a cry: "All my labor has been in vain," thought he, and was about to stop, but he heard the Bashkirs still shouting, and remembered that though to him, from below, the sun seemed to have set, they on the hillock could still see it. He took a long breath and ran up the hillock. It was still light there. He reached the top and saw the cap. Before it sat the Chief laughing and holding his sides. Again Pahom remembered his dream, and he uttered a cry: his legs gave way beneath him, he fell forward and reached the cap with his hands.

"Ah, what a fine fellow!" exclaimed the Chief. "He has gained much land!"

Pahom's servant came running up and tried to raise him, but he saw that blood was flowing from his mouth. Pahom was dead!

The Bashkirs clicked their tongues to show their pity.

His servant picked up the spade and dug a grave long enough for Pahom to lie in, and buried him in it. Six feet from his head to his heels was all he needed.

Printed in Great Britain
by Amazon

26902780R00030